Paul B. Janeczko

THAT
SWEET
DIAMOND

BASEBALL POEMS

illustrated by

CAROLE KATCHEN

Atheneum Books for Young Readers

BEFORE
the
GAME

Pennants wave
on the souvenir stand

Sausages snap,
sizzle with onions on the grill

Girls with mitts
practice catches to be made

Scorecard
Ohhh-ficial scorecard

Boys, wearing caps of faraway teams,
laugh, shove

Peanut shells crunch
underfoot

Cheese oozes
over nachos

Joy
thick as the perfume
of popcorn and
boiled hot dogs
fills the air

as
ticket takers call,
This way
This way to the game

the
BATTER

He approaches the plate,
ponderous,
swinging smoothly
in slow motion
knowing his choice is simple:
swing or
not.

As he paws
the back line of the batter's box,
matching concentration and stare
with the pitcher,
he knows
indecision
or
hesitation
makes failure likely.

Pitcher rocks.

Batter waits.

Then, in the time it takes
a happy heart to beat,
decides.

NICKNAMES

No one is happy
to be Bill or Brian or Joe.
Those are names
for teachers, parents, distant aunts.

Here
Bill is the Bopper,
Brian is Snake
(for build not deeds),
Joe, the pitcher, is, of course,
Gas.

The others—
Scooter, Hoot, and Toots
Whale, Spunky, Goofy—
know who's who,
celebrate themselves,
singing their names
till they fill the air
of sweet summer nights.

the
PITCHER

Standing
alone,
above the rest
in the center of the diamond,
his art is foolery,
casting a spell,
never showing the batter
more than he needs to know
for the moment
it takes a slider, change, or
tantalizing curve
to break the heart
of the plate.

VENDORS

An army of vendors
roams the stands—
red shirts,
narrow paper caps,
aprons for money—
lugging trays of waxy cups of soda
or tubs of popcorn.
Their eyes—
the eyes of spies—
scan the fans
looking for a sign of recognition,
answer their mates as if in code:
liiiiiice cream!
Getcher peanuts!
liiiiiice cream!
Getcher peanuts!
ignoring the battle
being waged
on the field of flawless green.

CATCHER

sings the

BLUES

Crouching low, I sing the blues
The aches are now a part of me
Blocking home, I sing the blues
O, the aches are now a part of me
Bruises, bumps, and scrapes
Have worn me down, can't you see?

My knees sing the blues
They sing 'em when I stoop and bend
My knees sing the blues
O, they sing 'em when I stoop and bend
They crunch, crackle, pop
The hurtful noises never end.

My fingers sing the blues
When I grip a ball or make a fist
O, my fingers sing the blues
When I grip a ball or make a fist
The knuckles moan and cry
By fire every one is kissed

Crouching low, I sing the blues
The aches are now a part of me
Blocking home, I sing the blues
O, these aches are now a part of me
Too many bruises, bumps, and scrapes
I'm nothing like I used to be.

No, nothing like I used to be

PRAYER

——————◆——————

for the

——————◆——————

UMPIRES

May you go unnoticed
in your job of noticing
things small and large:
the edges of the plate
as well as its heart,
the hands of the fans
eager for
a souvenir before its time,
the bounce of the ball
the lay of the line
the mutterings
of the sulky clean-up batter.

May your voice
leave no doubt
about ball or *stee-riiike.*

May your knees not ache.

May your arches not fall.

May your mask remain sound.

And may you give all players
their say
before you turn away.

the
INFIELD

Like the barnyard,
with the infielders
scratching
in the dust
with their toes;

walking
heads down
but with a watchful eye
on the umpire
ready to squawk.

And the chatter
batterbatterbatter
hummmm baby
no batterbatter.
Always the chatter.

A CURSE

upon the

PITCHER

Peanut shells, pigeon feather,
Dance a jig in stormy weather.
Ice cream stick, bubble gum,
Hurler, may you lose your hum.

HOW
to
SPIT

At the plate,
never without an attitude:
arrogance or annoyance.
Never as if you were just spitting.
And always for an audience.

Practice
is the key
to developing your style.

Check the wind.

Concentrate.

Don't dribble.

A spray is as pitiful
as fouling to the catcher.

Noise is optional.

Save the practical spit
for the pocket of your mitt.

SIGNS

The third-base coach
peers
shrugs
(scratches)
brushes his sleeves
encourages
claps
cheers
tugs one earlobe
then the other
whistles
(scratches)
exhorts
rubs his hands
hollers
paces
gazes
turns his back.

The batter
steps out:
he needs to see
them all
again.

FOUL
BALL

Sometimes
the play on the field is
ignored

as the ball bounces off
hands that want it too much

or scuttles
down a runway
quick as a rat
racing to its hiding place

or settles
in the grip of a woman
who holds her prize aloft
flashes a grin
as the fans—knowing her
only for her luck—
cheer
as if her catch
could somehow change the game.

#20998
$16.00

DOUBLE
PLAY

The runner is
a non-swimmer in deep water,
inching from the bag
timid
returning in alarm.

The shortstop and second baseman
are schoolboys
passing secrets
behind the pitcher's back.

Moving before the pitch,
the shortstop dashes to the bag
glove up in anticipation
as runner and
peg from his partner at second
approach.
He drags the toe of his right shoe
across the bag
as the ball slaps home
and he leaps
to avoid the spikes.

Resting in air
safely above the slide
long enough to throw to first
before he tumbles to the dirt,
his eyes on the ball
the mitt
until
the umpire's confirmation of perfection.

THINGS
TO DO
during a
RAIN
DELAY

Watch the puddles deepen in front
  of the dugouts.

Work your umbrella up   up
                      and   and
                        down   down.

Build a castle of used paper cups.

Count all the stairs
walk all the aisles
from left field to right.

Hold your umbrella   just   so
to let raindrops drip   off   the edge
onto the neck of the man in front of you.

Look away quickly when he turns.

SECTION 7, ROW 1, SEAT 3

She comes prepared.
From a tattered gym bag
she pulls
her game cushion,
worn to fit her,
binoculars,
a few chewed but sharp #2 pencils,
her own pad of score sheets,
and a flask of black coffee.

She measures life
in baseball time:
born the year Yankee Stadium opened,
married the summer of The Streak,
    Ted's .406,
son born during Jackie Robinson's
    first season,
daughter born two days after
the "shot heard 'round the world,"
alone since the Yankees' last pennant.

"Leaving before the last out,"
she says, resting her chin on her
    ebony cane,
"is like dying
before your time."

CENTER

FIELDER

The ball hawk patrols his green range—
eyes lost in the shadows
of the bill of his cap,
alert to small movements—
takes flight,
it seems,
as the ball leaves the pitcher,
before the quick music
of the crack of the bat
darts the ball
toward the emptiness behind him.

Betrayed by the wind this night,
the ball falls.
There is no escape.
The ball hawk seizes
it in his talon grip
and circles toward the dugout
as easily as thunder
rolling through a summer sky.

PLAY

— at the —

PLATE

Some
watch the ball
short hop the wall and
the right fielder—who can't
pick it up fast enough—
finally snatch it
sling it
to the impatient cut-off man,
who throws home
almost before he turns.

Some
watch the runner
barely
toe the inside corner of third,
eyes on
the coach's windmill arm
signaling haste.

All
watch the meeting place:
the catcher begging for the ball
so he can sweep the tag
at the runner beginning
his slide
before the umpire,
holding his mask
behind his back
as casually as a satin heart
of valentine candy,
signals the meeting over,
the runner safe.

NUNS

The nuns from Holy Name,
settled in a row
behind the first-base dugout
straight as piano keys,
began the game
with composure
and popcorn
from paper megaphones,
used by the third
to amplify their pleas.

In the fifth
all but two fell
victim to The Wave.

In the seventh
they stretched,
the click of their beads lost in
"Take Me Out to the Ball Game."

Faith
in their team
paid off
in the ninth
when the catcher with a saintly
swing
sent a pitch
to the gravel parking lot
behind the fence,
close enough to heaven
to win the game.

AFTER

the

GAME

Bases yanked.
Infield groomed.
Tarp pulled
to the edge of the outfield grass,
smoothed.
Lowered flags folded.
Hisst, hisst, hisst of brooms
sweeping aisles and ramps.

Section by section,
the lights go out
until the field is dark,
and the ghosts of players
gone
to other lives
long
for another game
on that sweet diamond.

For Linda Kucan and Roger Frank,
true friends and true baseball fans,
whose love of the game runs deeper
than their allegiance to a team
—P. B. J.

These paintings are dedicated to
the Arkansas Travelers, and all the
other minor league players who keep
baseball alive and accessible
for today's kids.
—C. K.

Atheneum Books for Young Readers
An imprint of Simon & Schuster
Children's Publishing Division
1230 Avenue of the Americas
New York, New York 10020

Book design by Nina Barnett

The text of this book is set in Folio.
The illustrations are rendered in pastels.

First Edition
Printed in Singapore
10 9 8 7 6 5 4 3 2 1

Library of Congress Cataloging-in-Publication Data
Janeczko, Paul B.
That sweet diamond : baseball poems / by Paul B.
Janeczko ; illustrated by Carole Katchen.—1st ed.
p.   cm.
Summary: A collection of poems—including "Before
the Game," "Catcher Sings the Blues," "How to
Spit," and "Double Play"—captures the experience
of the game of baseball.
ISBN 0-689-80735-X
1. Baseball—Juvenile poetry. 2. Children's
poetry, American.
[1. Baseball—Poetry. 2. American poetry.]
I. Katchen, Carole, ill. II. Title.
PS3560.A465T48   1998
811'.54—dc21
97-5044